W9-BEZ-104

Balzer + Bray is an imprint of HarperCollins Publishers.
Little Penguin Gets the Hiccups. Copyright © 2015 by Tadgh Bentley. All rights reserved. Printed in the United States of America. No part of this book may be used or reproduced in any manner whatsoever without written permission except in the case of brief quotations embodied in critical articles and reviews.
For information address HarperCollins Children's Books, a division of HarperCollins Publishers, 195 Broadway, New York, NY 10007.
www.harpercollinschildrens.com

ISBN 978-0-06-233536-4

Tadgh Bentley

Little Penguin gets the Hiccups

BALZER + BRAY
An Imprint of HarperCollins*Publishers*

CHEER
CHEER
CHEER

Oh, hello. It's so nice to HIC!
meet you. Franklin said you
would be here soon.

I wonder if you might be able to help. You may have noticed that HIC! I've got a terrible case of the HIC! hiccups. It's driving me cuckoo. It all started last week on HIC! chili night.

I'm not sure how many penguins you know, but let me give you some HIC! advice.

CHILI

NEV
give
to a

Chill
enguin.
It gives us HIC! hiccups.

I can't get rid of them. Frederick
HIC! told me to stand on my head.

Chester told me to HIC!
drink backward from a cup.

Albert told me to stand on my HIC!
head while drinking backward from a cup.

Nothing works.

But Franklin HIC! has given
me a new idea, and I need your help.

Apparently HIC! giving someone a good scare is the surest HIC! bestest way to cure hiccups.

SO I NEED YOU TO SCARE ME.

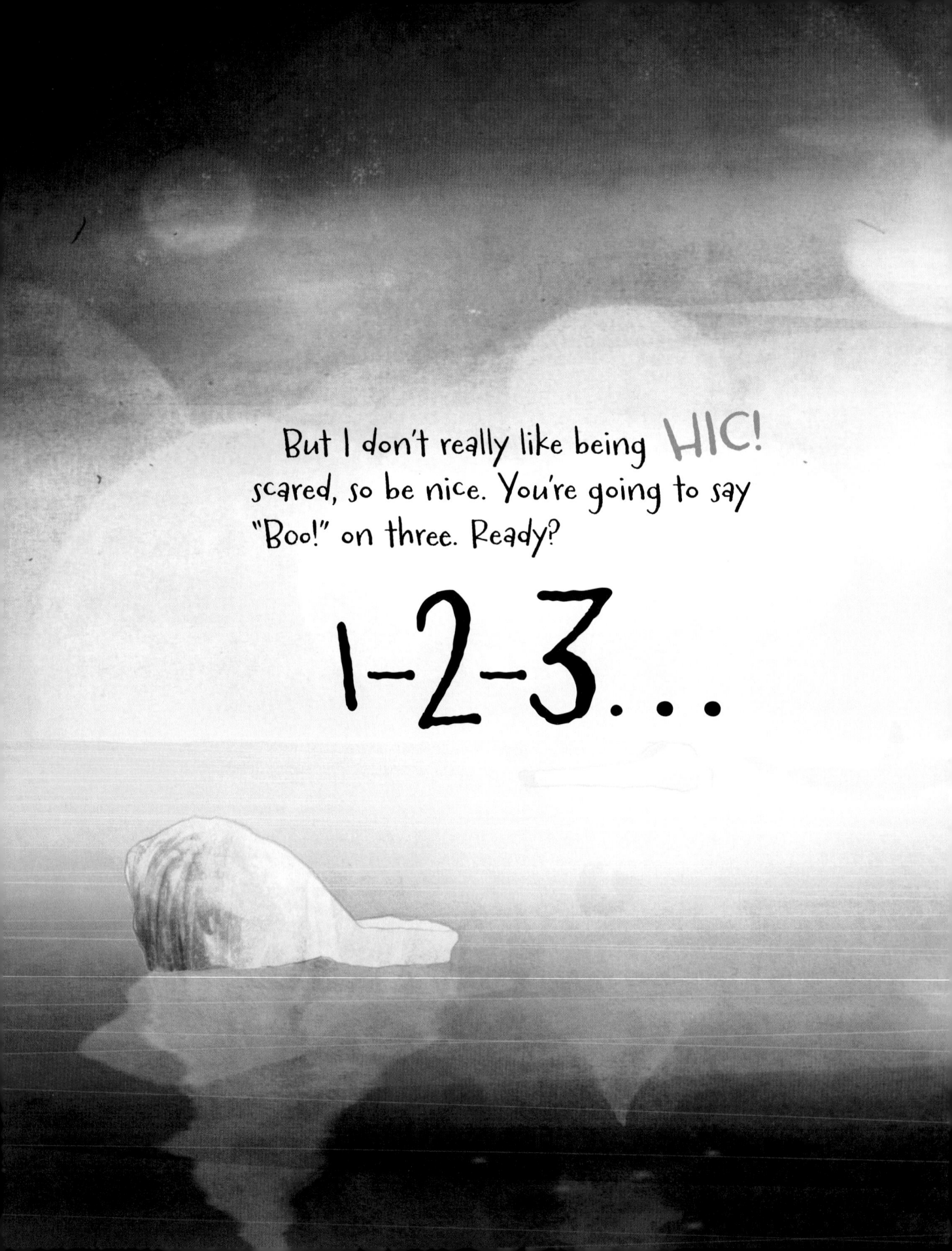

But I don't really like being HIC!
scared, so be nice. You're going to say
"Boo!" on three. Ready?

1-2-3...

BOO!

HIC!

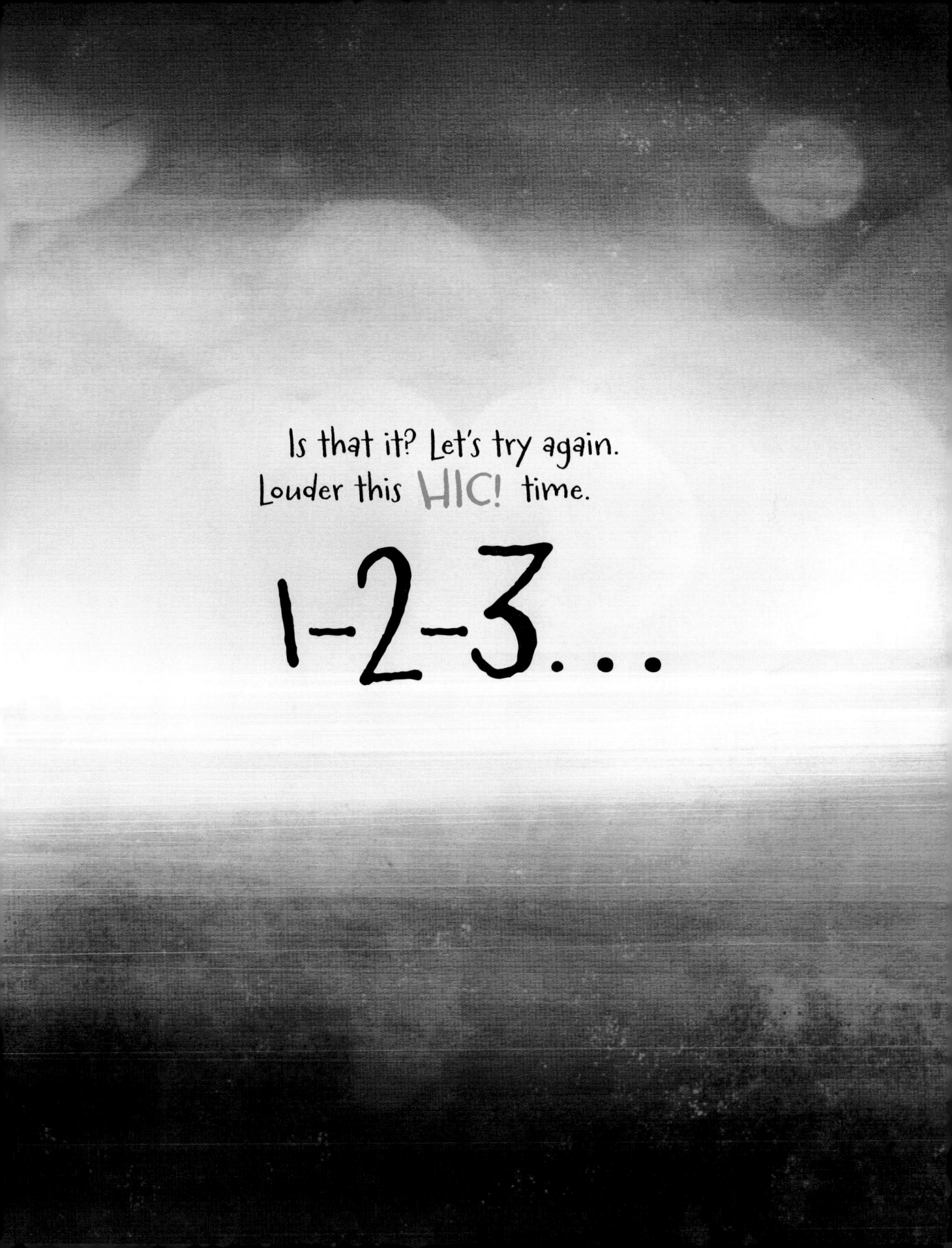
Is that it? Let's try again.
Louder this HIC! time.
1-2-3...

BOO!

Pretty scary! Maybe that cured my—

HIC!

ARRGH!
Will I have HIC! the hiccups forever?

One more time.
SHOUT!
GO CRAZY!

Ready?
1-2-3...

ROAR!

Franklin! What on earth are you doing? You told me to stand here and wait for a good scare and then you go and jump out on me so now my feathers are all wet and my mom will go BONKERS because she JUST washed these the other day. Now I'll have to wait until I'm ready to be scared again. . . .

My hiccups! They're gone!
Oh, thank you ever so much!

Let's celebrate with a nice spicy taco!

HIC!